The Little Green Drum

There are lots of Early Reader
stories you might enjoy.

Look at the back of the book or,
for a complete list, visit
www.orionbooks.co.uk

The Little Green Drum

Taghreed Najjar

Retold by Lucy Coats

Illustrated by Hassan Manasrah

Orion
Children's Books

Originally published in the Arabic language
in Jordan in 2013
by Al Salwa Publishers
This translated edition first published in Great Britain in 2015
by Orion Children's Books
an imprint of the Hachette Children's Group

Orion House
5 Upper Saint Martin's Lane
London WC2H 9EA
An Hachette UK Company

1 3 5 7 9 10 8 6 4 2

ISBN 978 1 4440 1435 8

A catalogue record for this book is available from the British Library.

Printed and bound in China

www.orionchildrensbooks.co.uk

Contents

Chapter One

This is Samia, and this is her dad, Yaba.

Samia and Yaba live in a village called Lifta. All the houses are on the side of a steep hill. Almost every house has a dome on top.

Samia thinks they look like friendly square giants wearing little round hats.

Samia and Yaba know everyone in
their village, and everyone knows
them. This is because Yaba has
a Very Important Job. He is the
Dawn Waker-Upper for the whole
village, during the holy month of
Ramadan.

During Ramadan, no one can eat
in the daytime – from when the
sun rises at dawn to when it sinks
at dusk. Instead, everyone must
have an early breakfast.

So Yaba marches around the
village in the dark, banging on his
drum and shouting:
   "Wake up! Wake up,
sleepyheads! It's time to eat!"

Samia is proud of Yaba and his
Very Important Job. She secretly
wishes she could march around
the village banging a drum and
shouting, just like him.

But when she asks Yaba about it, he laughs.

"There's never been a Dawn Waker-Upper who is a girl, my flower," he says. "Not that I've heard of, anyway."

Samia doesn't know why not. Girls are good at banging drums and shouting too, aren't they?

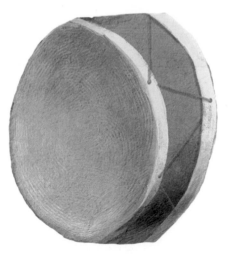

But one year, just before
Ramadan, Yaba is not very well.
"Ooh! Ow! Ouch! My poor
stomach!" he says. "I think I need
to lie down."

Samia brings him a cup of special tummy-ache tea.

"Drink up, Yaba," she says. "You have to be well for tomorrow! It's the first day of Ramadan."

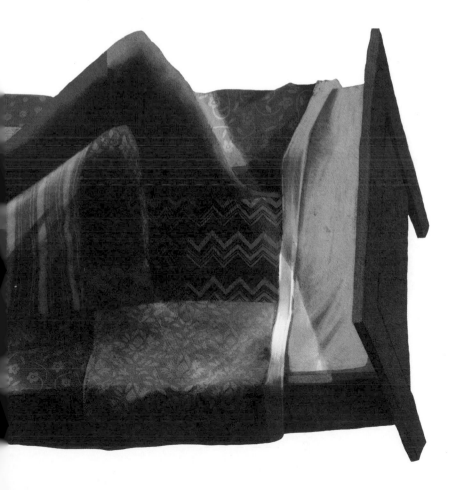

But Yaba doesn't feel better. He doesn't feel better **at all**. When he tries to get up, he falls back into bed, holding his tummy. It hurts more than ever.

"Oh no!" he moans. "Ramadan will be **ruined** if I don't wake everyone up!"

Chapter Two

"I can do it, Yaba," says Samia. "I'm strong and brave, and my little green drum is **very** loud."

"But won't you get lost in the dark?" Yaba asks.

"This lamp is as bright as the stars," says Samia. "It will show me the way."

"But what about the wild wolves?" asks Yaba. "They might eat you."

"Don't worry," says Samia.

"Our dog Barkie is as fierce as a wolf! He'll look after me.

So Yaba stays warm in his bed, and Samia sets off down the rocky road to the village with her little green drum, her bright lamp, and her fierce dog, Barkie.

It is very dark. Samia hums a tune
to help her feel brave, and holds
her lamp high. But then . . .

Oh no!

She sees two scary, orange eyes shining behind a tree.

What could they be?

Chapter Three

ARROOOOH! ARROOOOOOOH!

howls a big, black wolf.

WOOF! WOOF! WOOF! barks
Barkie. STAY AWAY FROM
SAMIA OR I'LL BITE YOU!

Barkie's growls are so fierce that
the big, black wolf runs away.

"Good dog, Barkie!" says
Samia, stroking his soft, brown
ears. "I knew you'd save me."

She holds up her lamp, and off they go again.

Soon Samia reaches her friend Ahmad's house. She bangs on her little green drum, just like Yaba. Will it work? It must!

BOOM
-A-
BOOM

"Wake up, wake up, sleepyheads! It's time to eat!" she shouts in a loud voice.

Ahmad's dad looks out of the bedroom window.

"Well, I never!" he says. "It's Samia! Where is your Yaba?"

"Yaba is ill and can't get out of bed" says Samia. "So I am taking his place as Dawn Waker-Upper."

"Ooh!" says Ahmad, popping up next to his dad. "I've got a drum.

Can I come too?"

"And me!"

"And me!" say Ahmad's sisters, Ada and Arya.

So Ahmad, Ada and Arya join
Samia and Barkie.

BOOM-A-BOOM
BOOM-A-BOOM

"Wake up, wake up sleepyheads!
It's time to eat!" they shout.

Chapter Four

Their friend Omar wants to come too.

"I don't have a drum. Can I bring my tambourine?" he asks.

"Why not?" everyone yells.
"Five are louder than four!"

So Omar joins Samia, Barkie,
Ahmad, Ada and Arya.
"Wake up, wake up
sleepyheads! It's time to eat!"
they shout.

42

BOOM-A-BOOM BOOM-A-BOOM JINGLE JANGLE

The next house is Fatima's.
"I don't have a drum or a
tambourine. Can I bring my
flute?" she asks.

"Why not?" everyone yells.

"Six are louder than five!"

So Fatima joins Samia, Barkie, Ahmad, Ada, Arya and Omar.

BOOM-A-BOOM
BOOM-A-BOOM
JINGLE JANGLE
TOOTLE TOOT

"Wake up, wake up sleepyheads! It's time to eat!" they shout.

"Ooh!" says Adnan when they get to his house.

"I don't have a drum or a tambourine or a flute. Can I bring my lute?"

"Why not?" everyone yells. "Seven are louder than six!"

So Adnan joins Samia, Barkie, Ahmad, Ada, Arya, Omar and Fatima.

BOOM-A-BOOM
BOOM-A-BOOM
JINGLE JANGLE
TOOTLE TOOT
PLINKETY
PLINK

"Wake up, wake up sleepyheads!
It's time to eat!" they shout.

Bahira and Samira are not sure
what to bring.
"How about saucepans and
spoons?" they ask.

"Why not?" everyone yells. "Nine are loudest of all!"

So Bahira and Samira join Samia, Barkie, Ahmad, Ada, Arya, Omar, Fatima and Adnan.

BOOM-A-BOOM
BOOM-A-BOOM
JINGLE JANGLE
TOOTLE TOOT

PLINKETY PLINK BASHETTY BISH

"Wake up, wake up sleepyheads!
It's time to eat!" they shout.

Chapter Five

Soon Samia has a whole band.

Up and down the village they march, banging and beating, plucking and playing, tooting and hooting.

Then they start to sing.

Bang the drum
along the way
Here we come
Before the day!

Let's give food to everyone,
Eat your meal
Before the sun.
Ramadan is here, hooray!
We must eat before the day!

"Surely nobody can still be
asleep now!" says Samia, giving
her little green drum one last
boom-a-boom to make sure.

Her friends look around. There is a
light on in every house.

Everyone in the village is awake.

"Happy Ramadan!" Samia shouts.

"Yes! Happy Ramadan to all the Dawn Waker-Uppers!" say the mums and dads, grannies and granddads, aunties, uncles and cousins.

Samia, Ahmad, Ada, Arya, Omar,
Fatima, Adnan, Bahira and
Samira are given lots of treats.

Samia looks at the sky. The stars are fading. It is nearly dawn.

"I must go home to Yaba," she says. "I hope his tummy-ache has gone."

She waves goodbye to everyone, and she, her little green drum, her bright lamp and her fierce dog, Barkie, walk back up the rocky road.

65

The big, black wolf is hiding
behind a tree. He doesn't dare
to come out. Barkie wags his tail
happily. He is the Dog King of the
village now.

Samia runs into the house.

Yaba is sitting up in bed. He looks much better.

"Welcome home, flower," he says, hugging her. "Is everyone awake?"

"Oh yes, Yaba!" Samia says. "And guess what happened?"

"You'll have to tell me," Yaba says.

So Samia does.

"Happy Ramadan to the best Dawn Waker-Upper in the village," says Yaba, as he and Samia sit down to eat.

"Happy Ramadan to the best Yaba in the whole WORLD," says Samia.

70

Samia's story happened a long time ago in 1930s Palestine in a village called Lifta. In 1948, there was a war and the villagers of Lifta had to flee to a safer place. When the war ended the villagers were not allowed to return to their homes and today the village still stands empty and unlived in. Taghreed Najjar's family came from Lifta, and she wrote this story in memory of peaceful and happier times there.

In those days, nobody had an alarm clock, so when the holy month of Ramadan came around, every village relied on their Mosaher, or Dawn Waker-Upper to get them up for the early morning meal, which is called Suhoor.

During Ramadan, which falls in the ninth month of the Islamic year, nobody eats between the time the sun rises and sets, so getting a big breakfast in is very important. Muslims also have a Ramadan meal after dark, which is called Iftar.

The end of Ramadan is marked by a big celebration called Eid-ul-Fitr, when Muslims thank Allah for the help and strength that he gives them throughout the month of fasting.

What are you going to read next?

Have more adventures with
Horrid Henry,

or save the day with Anthony Ant!

Become a
superhero with Monstar,

float off to
sea with
Algy,

or have your very own Pirates' Picnic.

Grow carrots with

Lottie and Dottie,

make magic with The Witch Dog,

and cast a spell with The Three Little Magicians.

Enjoy all the Early Readers.

the orion star

CALLING ALL GROWN-UPS!
Sign up for **the orion star** newsletter to
hear about your favourite authors and exclusive
competitions, plus details of how children
can join our 'Story Stars' review panel.

Sign up at:

www.orionbooks.co.uk/orionstar

Follow us 🐦 @the_orionstar
Find us [f] facebook.com/TheOrionStar